PUMP POW

PATRICIA CLEVELAND-PECK

ILLUSTRATED BY HANNAH MARKS

BLOOMSBURY EDUCATION

BLOOMSBURY EDUCATION
Bloomsbury Publishing Plc
50 Bedford Square, London, WC1B 3DP, UK

BLOOMSBURY, BLOOMSBURY EDUCATION and the Diana logo are
trademarks of Bloomsbury Publishing Plc

First published in Great Britain 2019 by Bloomsbury Publishing Plc
Text copyright © Patricia Cleveland-Peck, 2019
Illustrations copyright © Hannah Marks, 2019

Patricia Cleveland-Peck and Hannah Marks have asserted their rights under the Copyright,
Designs and Patents Act, 1988, to be identified as Author and Illustrator of this work

A catalogue record for this book is available from the British Library

ISBN: PB: 978-1-4729-6119-8; ePDF: 978-1-4729-6118-1; ePub: 978-1-4729-6117-4;
enhanced ePub: 978-1-4729-6953-8

2 4 6 8 10 9 7 5 3 1

Printed and bound in China by Leo Paper Products, Heshan, Guangdong

To find out more about our authors and books visit www.bloomsbury.com
and sign up for our newsletters

Chapter One

Once upon a time there was a young boy called Perkin. He worked as a gardener for a very rich old man.

This old man had just got married for the second time and his new wife was a nasty, mean woman. She had never had a garden before, let alone a gardener, and she didn't know how to treat either.

She made poor Perkin work too hard for too little money and so he never had enough to eat.

Chapter Two

One day Perkin was weeding near the front door when it opened and a strange woman came walking down the path.

"Hello," she called out. "I've just been to visit my poor god-daughter. She's been so unhappy since her mother died. Still, they have a lovely garden. How lucky you are to work in such a beautiful place."

7

In fact Perkin didn't feel lucky. He felt fed up, tired and hungry.

The woman looked at him more closely. "What's the problem?" she asked. She opened her big bag and took out a bar of chocolate. She broke it in two and offered Perkin half.

As he ate his chocolate Perkin found himself telling her how hard he had to work and how he felt hungry most of the time.

The woman thought for a minute.

Then she delved into her bag again and brought out a little paper bag.

Inside were some seeds. Big seeds.
She counted out seven of these seeds
and gave them to Perkin.
"Find a corner out of sight and clear the
ground," she said.

"Plant these and water them and in one hundred days you'll have food enough." With this she shut her bag and swept out of the gate.

11

Chapter Three

Perkin did as she told him. Very soon, each seed sent up two leaves.
Then two more, then two more and then, to Perkin's surprise, the plants began to spread out all over the patch.

Next Perkin saw flowers beginning to grow on the plants.

Then, at the base of each flower, a fruit began to swell up.

Soon the whole piece of ground was covered with red, orange, yellow, green, pink, blue and golden fruits. Some were oval, some round like footballs, some long like bananas.

Chapter Four

So far this little patch of garden had been Perkin's secret but he had one friend, Cindy, the daughter of the owner and his first wife. She had to work as hard inside as Perkin did outside and she too was always hungry.

One day Perkin showed her his secret
garden.

"Perkin, how clever you are to have grown
all this!" she said.
Perkin was happy but a bit embarrassed.
"But what are they?" he asked.
"Pumpkins, they're pumpkins," she
replied. "Fancy you, a gardener, not
knowing!" she laughed, but not unkindly.

"Do you know how to cook them?"
he asked.
"I'll soon find out," she answered.
So when the one hundred days were up
Perkin began to cut the pumpkins and
bring them to the house.

Cindy, who was a very good cook,
secretly made pumpkin soup, roast
pumpkin, pumpkin pie, pumpkin cakes,
pumpkin scones and pumpkin jams.
For the first time neither she nor Perkin
was hungry.

Chapter Five

One evening they were sitting in the kitchen.
"You don't look very happy tonight," said Perkin. "What's the matter?"
"Well," replied Cindy, "if you must know, they've all gone out to a big party. My father, my step-mother and my two step-sisters…"

"I call them the ugly sisters," said Perkin. This brought a smile to Cindy's face. "But as usual I was left out," she said and her eyes filled with tears. "And I should so like to go."

At that moment the back door flew open and there stood the woman who had given Perkin the seeds.

"My goodness, Godmother," exclaimed Cindy. "What are you doing here?"

"You shall go to the party, Cinderella," said her godmother.

"But how on earth could I possibly get there in time?" asked Cindy. "They left ages ago."

"Pumpkin Power," replied the godmother, giving Perkin a big wink. She turned to him and said, "Run and fetch me your biggest and best pumpkin."

He hurried back with his fattest
pumpkin and the godmother
waved a wand and turned the
pumpkin into a super-fast car.

Then she changed the mice, the rats and the lizards into a chauffeur, bodyguards and people to help Cindy get ready.

Finally she changed Cindy's tatty old jeans into a marvellous designer dress and her scuffed trainers into a pair of sparkly shoes.

"Be sure to be back by midnight," called the godmother as Cindy set off.

Then the godmother and Perkin settled down to a cosy evening of looking at pumpkin catalogues.

Chapter Six

You've probably heard what happened next: how at the party the Prince fell in love with Cinderella, how she lost one of her glass shoes and how the Prince eventually found her – much to the annoyance of her step-mother and the ugly sisters.

That however, was not quite the end of the story. Cindy got to know the Prince and eventually they fell in love and got married but soon afterwards the Prince was tricked out of all his money (by those ugly sisters in fact). Although he tried, he couldn't get a job. So he and Cindy were quite poor.

Perkin meanwhile had continued in the pumpkin business and was doing well. Cindy and he often met and talked and one day Perkin told Cindy that although each year he sold more pumpkins and bought more land and by now had a fleet of lorries – there was a problem.

Pumpkins did not grow all year round.
Then Cindy, who was a very clever girl,
had an idea.

"Perkin, do you remember what we did
when we were hungry?" she asked.

"Yes," replied Perkin. "You made soup
and biscuits and…"

"... cakes, and scones and pumpkin pies," continued Cindy. "Well we could do that again and have things to sell all year round."

"What a brilliant idea," said Perkin. "And you and the Prince could be my business partners."

Now you may never have heard of the company Cindy, Perkin & Prince but I bet you've tasted their soup or eaten one of their biscuits.

So like in all good stories they all lived happily ever after but none of them ever forgot that their good fortune depended on something as down to earth as seven pumpkin seeds.